Voices of
Feminism

Voices of Feminism

PAST, PRESENT, AND FUTURE

JoAnn Bren Guernsey

LERNER PUBLICATIONS COMPANY
MINNEAPOLIS, MINNESOTA

Library of Congress Cataloging-in-Publication Data

Guernsey, JoAnn Bren.
    Voices of feminism / JoAnn Bren Guernsey.
        p.   cm.
    Includes index.
    Summary: Traces the development of the feminist movement from the eighteenth century to the 1990s, discussing such topics as women and the vote, men's rights, and power feminism.
    ISBN 0-8225-2626-3
    1. Feminism—Juvenile literature. [1. Feminism. 2. Women—Suffrage. 3. Women—Employment.] I. Title.
    HQ1154.G8 1996
    305.42—dc20   95-12683

Manufactured in the United States of America
1 2 3 4 5 6 - S - 01 00 99 98 97 96

Contents

As the feminist movement has evolved, some people have embraced it—and others have resented it.

1
FEAR OF FEMINISM

School is out for the day, but a handful of students gather in a classroom to talk. One of the girls relates an incident from lunch when a tableful of boys taunted her about the size of her breasts. Another says she hardly ever gets called on or recognized by her calculus teacher. Still another wants to discuss contraception.

This group calls itself a women's issues club. It is one of many such groups in junior and senior high schools across the United States. In many cases, these young women (and men) are not afraid to draw attention to themselves; but in other cases the groups meet quietly, almost secretively. Why? Because they fear being labeled feminists.

The image of feminists who gathered on college campuses during the turbulent 1960s and 1970s is one of confident agitators. It's a picture of unity and purpose. But during the 1980s and 1990s, public opinion changed, and being identified as a feminist carried risks. Feminist activists at Duke University, for example, received obscene phone calls; hecklers disrupted an antirape march at Princeton University; and vandals slashed the picture of a woman's body displayed on advertisements for "Women's Weekend" at the University of Michigan.[1]

These incidents represent an intolerance of feminism—a term that is generally defined as a movement to secure economic, social, and political rights for women equal to those enjoyed by men. If young women of the 1990s still don't quite have equality, is that because as a society, people oppose it, or because they oppose the feminist movement? Is feminism part of the problem rather than part of the solution?

The history of feminism is long and complex. For more than 150 years, voices from all over the world have cried out on behalf of women's rights. Defining the movement requires sorting through the rich variety of those voices. In 1913, for instance, author Rebecca West admitted that she never figured out exactly what feminism was. "I only know," she wrote, "that people call me a feminist whenever I express sentiments that differentiate me from a doormat."[2]

One of the strongest young voices of the 1990s, Katie Roiphe, remembers that "when I was very young I thought of feminism as something like a train you could catch and ride to someplace better. My grandmother missed it, but my mother caught it."[3] And another young leader, Heather Stein, of WIN (Women's Information Network), says, "There are as many ways to be a feminist today as there are women."[4]

Critics of feminism provide their own definitions. Perhaps one of the most extreme critics is conservative, right-wing leader Pat Robertson. In one fund-raising letter to voters, he called feminism "a socialist antifamily political movement that encourages women to leave

Right-wing leader Pat Robertson called feminism "a socialist antifamily political movement."

their husbands, kill their children, practice witchcraft, destroy capitalism and become lesbians."[5]

The belief in fairness is the idea that underlies feminism. Yet when attitudes and behavior are examined more closely, some surprising conflicts appear. Although the idea of *fairness* usually appeals to people, the idea of *feminism* often does not. Feminists are sometimes accused of hating men. At other times, they are accused of wanting to be just like men. Feminists are alternately accused of having a hunger for power and an obsession with being victims. And many people who say they believe in equality mean only up to a point. They draw the line, for instance, at the idea of women being drafted into military combat, or granting child custody to an equal number of fathers as mothers after divorce.

Some people believe mothers, not fathers, should receive custody of their children following a divorce. Here, some fathers fight back.

Research during the early part of the 1990s consistently showed that most women support the women's rights agenda, but far fewer are willing to identify themselves as feminists. In one widely publicized poll reported in February 1992 by *Time*/CNN, for example, 82 percent of the women contacted said they had more freedom than their mothers did, 39 percent said the women's movement had improved their lives, and 57 percent said there was still a need for a strong women's movement. Did these women consider themselves feminists? A surprising 63 percent said no.[6]

Typical negative answers to the question "Are you a feminist?" include views that feminists hate men and heterosexual contact, overreact to everything, whine a lot, are an "insider" group of mostly upper-income white women, and contribute to the notion that women are the weaker sex—in need of special treatment.

Perhaps the most disturbing answer to the question "Are you a feminist?" is *"Who cares?"* This answer comes from people with widely divergent viewpoints. Some people, for instance, say they don't care because the women's movement has achieved its goals. After all, we now have female doctors, lawyers, construction workers, astronauts, even Supreme Court justices. Others say they don't care about feminism because they believe women don't want equality. For some women, the traditional female role—being financially supported by a man in exchange for nurturing children and managing a household—is more natural, comfortable, and safe.

Revolution

Feminist pioneer Gloria Steinem—perhaps the one woman most identified with the movement—says, "The real opposition comes when you say, 'I'm a feminist, I'm for equal power for all women,' which is a revolution, instead of 'I'm for equal rights for me,' which is a reform."[7] Steinem understands this preference for reform over revolution, but she presses for revolution anyway. "We don't just want to have a piece of the pie," she says. "We want to make a whole new pie."[8]

But not everyone can follow her confident lead. Lisa Maria Hogeland, a University of Cincinnati women's studies professor, wrote an essay entitled "Fear of Feminism" for *Ms.* magazine after facing her students in the fall of 1994. She offers several reasons why many young women reject feminism, including fear of politics, of commitment, and of living with the consequences of one's actions.

Hogeland points out that powerful elements in American society are set firmly against feminism. And many young people want to avoid anger, resist change, and just be left alone. Hogeland says that many women "fear taking a public stand, entering public discourse, demanding —and perhaps getting—attention. And for what? To be called a 'feminazi'? To be denounced as traitors to women's 'essential nature'?"[9]

Perhaps it is the media-hyped images of feminism that are most to blame for its rejection. While doing research for her book *Fire with Fire: The New Female Power and How It Will Change the 21st Century,* author Naomi Wolf interviewed many young women. She was appalled to find that, to many of them, "the main thing that determines feminism is body hair."[10]

It hasn't helped the movement's image to be commonly identified with a few radical voices whose positions tend to be oversimplified. Extremist messages play well in the media. It is widely reported, for instance, that feminist writer Susan Brownmiller considers all men rapists and that radical activist Andrea Dworkin claims all heterosexual intercourse is rape. But what else have these women said and written? Dworkin and lawyer-activist Catherine MacKinnon advocate censorship

When the news agency UPI took this photo of Gloria Steinem in 1972, it called her a "women's lib leader."

because they blame pornography for inciting men to violence against women. And the media sometimes makes it seem that all feminists cry out for abortion on demand.

Because of all the disagreement about how to approach women's rights, many feminists warn against losing sight of what they see as the most dramatic change in the lives of young women during the late 20th century: for most women, marriage is no longer a career choice. With a shaky economy and soaring divorce rates, women must adjust to the fact that they cannot count on the financial support of a man, either for themselves or for their children. Those feminists who focus too heavily on sexual issues such as rape, harassment, and pornography are likely to lose the support of the women whose main concern is economic survival.[11]

To the young woman trying to find her way in the world, being a feminist may seem to pose a high risk of rejection, especially from men. According to Hogeland, "Young women may believe that a feminist identity puts them out of the pool for many men, limits the options of who they might become with a partner, and how they might decide to live."[12]

If the young feminist's relationship with men seems at risk, so does her sense of belonging with other

Each generation of women has had to redefine feminist goals.

women. During the 1970s, women celebrated their "sisterhood" with one another. But, as pointed out by feminist writer Susan Faludi, with the 1980s came a dramatic loss of collective spirit in the feminist movement. Women at home and in the workforce found themselves feeling alone and powerless. Faludi writes:

> When one is feeling stranded, finding a safe harbor inevitably becomes a more compelling course than bucking social currents. Keeping the peace with the particular man in one's life becomes more essential than battling the mass male culture. Saying one is "not a feminist" (even while supporting quietly every item of the feminist platform) seems the most prudent, self-protective strategy. Ultimately in such conditions, the impulse to remedy social injustice can become not only secondary but silent. [13]

Many leaders in the movement, however, are not particularly worried about the next generation of feminists. Gloria Steinem says, "I wasn't a feminist in my 20s either." She has observed that men tend to become more conservative as they get older, but "it's always been the older women who are more radical than the younger women." [14]

A New Surge of Activism
Young women of the 1990s grew up taking equality somewhat for granted. Women have made dramatic progress since the 1950s. But after the "backlash" decade of the 1980s, complacency began to give way to a new surge of feminism in which young women vowed to finish the work started, but left incomplete, by their mothers.

Even on many college campuses, women have to work harder than men to be taken seriously and to win prestigious grants and fellowships. On the job, a woman's pay in comparison to her male counterpart's has risen steadily since the 1970s, but women still earn approximately 70 to 75 cents for every dollar earned by men. And pay is not the only issue in the workplace.

Members of Chicago Women in Trades—who work as pipe fitters, electricians, laborers, and elevator repairers—say the harassment and sexual innuendos are relentless. They tell stories of foremen who withhold high-paying overtime work from women and of some men deliberately giving women wrong information during training. And often the women's bathroom is almost inaccessible. "The media may have shut up about discrimination, but we're still fighting the same. . . as we did before," says Wanda Griffin, a pipe fitter who makes $23.80 an hour.[15]

And what about the difficulty many women have in moving up into top management jobs? Feminists refer to a "glass ceiling" when they point to various subtle but seemingly impenetrable barriers to promotion. A 1995 report, the federal government's first comprehensive study, showed that women and minorities still have a long way to go for equality. White men constitute about 43 percent of the workforce but hold about 95 percent of senior management positions (defined as vice president and above).[16] Of the working poor, 65 percent are women. And single women head the majority of homeless families.[17]

At home and in their everyday lives, women still face barriers as well. Many—perhaps most—men are sensitive to women's issues and support their wives' and daughters' battles for equality. But it is still rare for a husband and wife who both work outside the home to share *equally* in child care and household duties. It is still common for a woman who is buying a car to face insulting questions from a salesperson who assumes that a husband or father must be part of the decision and the credit application. And a woman living alone still fears for her safety.

But if many problems persist, the nature of the feminist attack on them is evolving. A diverse group of young feminists is reshaping the movement, ridding themselves of many of the image problems suffered by earlier feminists (although inevitably battling some negative images of their own). They intend to break down the remaining barriers—including violence, poverty, homophobia (a dislike of homosexuals), and racism—to a higher quality of life for women and men alike.

As the editors of *Ms.* wrote in celebrating the feminist magazine's 22nd anniversary issue: "The beauty of this movement of ours is that it's so fluid—ever moving, evolving, growing. We are all changemakers seeking to make this a better world."[18]

2
THE FIRST 150 YEARS

H istory provides many examples of individual women with extraordinary power, courage, and talent. Such celebrities of women's history include empresses and queens, warriors, saints, martyrs, and artists. Joan of Arc, Pocahontas, Queen Elizabeth I, Florence Nightingale, Annie Oakley, and Louisa May Alcott come to mind. These women were exceptional, but they did not significantly improve the status of women in general.

Feminism was born when women began—as an organized group—to examine their roles in all spheres of life. They began to question the social institutions and value systems that had been designed and dominated by men, and that treated women as oppressed, second-class citizens.[1]

Many historians say that women's unequal status dates back to primitive societies and was based on a division of labor. Men were the hunters and warriors, while women served the domestic needs of their husbands and children. But the plight of women seemed to worsen dramatically during the 18th and 19th centuries.

It took great courage in the 1700s to rebel against the expectation that women stay home and be silent. In England, Mary Wollstonecraft (1759-97) was among the first

Women such as Joan of Arc made remarkable contributions long before feminism began.

women with such courage, and she became a founding mother of feminism. Mary was determined, despite the obstacles, to live a full and active life as an independent woman. Her determination grew when she met Joseph Johnson, a London publisher who championed the cause of all the oppressed. Mary became a central member of

Johnson's circle of friends in 1788, meeting regularly with other radical writers such as William Wordsworth, William Blake, and Thomas Paine.[2]

In 1792, Mary wrote a 300-page appeal, *A Vindication of the Rights of Woman*. This book was one of the first to claim that women should have equality with men. It became a best-seller and the foundation of modern feminism. Wollstonecraft declared, "It is time to restore women to their lost dignity and to make them part of the human race."[3] And "I do earnestly wish to see the distinction of sex abolished altogether . . . save where love is concerned."[4] Unfortunately, Wollstonecraft died young, during childbirth in 1797.[5]

One of the earliest American female rebels was Abigail Adams (1744–1818). She was the wife of John Adams (the second U.S. president) and the mother of John Quincy Adams (the sixth president). In letters to her husband while he was at the Continental Congress planning for a new American republic, Abigail suggested that the

Mary Wollstonecraft wrote *A Vindication of the Rights of Woman* in 1792.

new code of laws must forbid husbands unlimited power over wives, because "all men would be tyrants if they could." She further warned, "If particular care and attention is not paid to the Ladies, we are determined to foment a Rebellion, and will not hold ourselves bound by any laws in which we have no voice or Representatives."[6]

The field of education became one of the earliest arenas for the equal rights battle. In 1821, educator Emma Willard defied taboos against girls studying "manly" subjects such as math and science. She founded the Troy Female Seminary in New York state, giving girls a free high school education equal to that of boys. Frances Wright, a Scottish-American reformer, was one of the first American women to speak out effectively in public for women's rights. Her main focus was on equality in educational opportunities.[7]

Until the mid-19th century, many women had been working together with their husbands on farms. But the spread of manufacturing industries lured more and more people to the growing cities. Women and children earned only a fraction of men's wages, which helped create the ideal of the male "breadwinner" and the economically dependent "housewife."[7]

The Fight for Freedom

It was, however, the abolitionist (antislavery) movement that gave women—black and white—the first opportunity to organize politically against their own oppression. They banded together in 1837 at the first national antislavery convention in New York. Black women, such as Harriet Tubman, had been active in defying laws and freeing slaves, and suddenly women's political activity seemed more possible and respectable. Among the prominent feminist abolitionists were Lucy Stone, Angelina and Sarah Grimké, Lucretia Mott, Elizabeth Cady Stanton, and Susan B. Anthony.

While these women battled slavery, it was a natural step to push further for themselves, for freedom from male domination. Their passion for this cause became intensified in 1840 when Mott and Stanton, along with other American delegates, attended a World Antislavery Convention in London. The women were humiliated and enraged when the convention voted to seat only male delegates. Restricted to the viewing galleries for 10 days, Mott and Stanton vowed to fight for women's right to full equality with men.[8]

In 1848 feminist leaders organized the first Women's Rights Convention at Seneca Falls, New York. Delegates demanded not only women's suffrage (the right to vote), but also equality between husbands and wives. The convention focused on changing social policy laws because, at that time, life for the average American woman was not unlike slavery.

The story of Hester Vaughan provides a good example. In 1869, at the age of 20, after being deserted by her husband, she worked for a wealthy Philadelphia man who raped her. When she became pregnant, he fired her. Destitute and alone, Hester gave birth and immediately collapsed. The baby died. When Hester was charged with murder, no lawyer represented her, and she was not permitted to testify at her own trial. An all-male jury sentenced her to death.

Elizabeth Cady Stanton and Susan B. Anthony learned of Hester's tragic story and organized a campaign to help her. They staged protests, drawing hundreds of women. Eventually Stanton and Anthony won a pardon for Hester. They further demanded an end to the practice of judging a woman more harshly than a man for sexual behavior, and they insisted that women be allowed to serve as jurors and become lawyers. Their actions initiated a gradual change in the laws.[9]

Meanwhile, other doors were being pushed open. Thanks to Elizabeth Blackwell, America's first female doctor, all professions appeared less forbidden to women. Blackwell was rejected by 29 medical schools, but she finally forced her way into one and ignored the taunts from male students. She graduated at the head of her class and received her M.D. degree in 1849. When patients refused to consult her and hospitals refused to allow her to practice, she opened the New York Infirmary for Women and Children in 1857 with an all-woman staff. She went on to establish medical schools for women.[10]

In 1851 a powerful new voice emerged during a Women's Rights Convention in Akron, Ohio. Sojourner Truth was a freed slave, mother, and activist. When a clergyman in the audience insisted that women were too helpless to be allowed to vote, Sojourner rose to respond:

> The man over there says women need to be helped into carriages and lifted over ditches, and have the best places everywhere. Nobody ever helps me into carriages or over puddles, or gives me the best place—and ain't I a woman? Look at my arm! I have ploughed and planted and gathered into barns, and no man could head me—and ain't I a woman? I could work as much and eat as much as a man—when I could get it—and bear the lash as well. And ain't I a woman?[11]

Susan B. Anthony, *left,* and Elizabeth Cady Stanton, *right,* worked tirelessly in the early women's rights movement.

Two of the most outspoken feminist leaders, Anthony and Stanton, were instantly drawn to each other. They became best friends and ultimately worked together for women's rights for 50 years. Throughout the 1850s and 1860s, Susan was the organizer while Elizabeth, who had eight children, wrote the speeches. The two women shared child care and housekeeping chores, since Elizabeth's husband, a politician, was often absent.

Anthony and Stanton spoke tirelessly at meetings all over the country. Audiences often pelted them with rotten eggs and vegetables, jeers, and obscene language. Their goals included improved conditions for female teachers and the rights of married women to their own wages and property. And, of course, they campaigned for the right to vote.[12]

In those pre-Civil War years, a woman who stood up to speak in public was considered outrageous. If a woman had something to say to an audience, she was supposed to find a man to speak for her, or keep her thoughts to herself. But early feminists found various ways around this rule. According to Ann Braude, a professor of religious studies at Macalester College, the 19th-century Spiritualist movement gave many women the voice they needed.

Spiritualism was the popular belief, beginning in the late 1840s, that spirits of the dead could speak through the living. Many people, especially men, believed that when a woman became outspoken and full of ideas, spirits were speaking through her. As Spiritualists, then, women had a reason and permission to speak in public. Braude says about 200 such women traveled across the country, convincing audiences that they could go into trances through which the dead would speak.

These early Spiritualists gave long speeches that allowed them, according to Braude, "to cut through the authority of the church, clergy, even the Bible. They challenged slaveholders' power over slaves, husbands' [power] over wives. It was a transitional moment in women finding their own voice."[13] Many leaders in the suffrage movement were Spiritualists who made use of the religion to express their views.

Suffragists

The word *feminist* first appeared in a book review in the *Athenaeum* of April 27, 1895. The word described a woman who "has in her the capacity of fighting her way back to independence."[14] But the term was not widely used by the public until about 1910 when women's rights activists made the issue of suffrage a national campaign.

Alice Paul was an American Quaker who had studied and become a political activist in England. In 1913 Paul organized American suffragists into a group later known as the National Woman's Party. To campaign for the vote, this group used radical tactics such as chaining themselves to the White House fence. When arrested, these suffragists went on hunger strikes in jail, and then made more headlines when they were force-fed by police.[15]

When World War I began, women's right to the vote was reinforced by their war effort. With so many men going to war, women substituted for them in factories, offices, and public jobs. Suffragists argued that women were proving themselves the equals of men in both work and patriotic service, and they demanded to vote as fully participating citizens. On January 10, 1918, the Nineteenth Amendment, giving women the right to vote, was introduced into the House of Representatives. On August 26, 1920, it was finally ratified into law.

Not satisfied to rest on the laurels of that victory, Paul went on to campaign for the Equal Rights Amendment, which guaranteed total equality between men and women in every aspect of American life. She continued to fight for the amendment until 1977, when she died at the age of 92. The ERA was first introduced in Congress as early as 1923 by Representative Daniel Anthony, Susan Anthony's nephew. The amendment eventually passed in 1972, but the states didn't ratify it, so it failed as a constitutional amendment.[16]

Many people felt women had won equality when they

Onlookers applauded as the banner of the National Woman's Party was unfurled at its headquarters in Washington, D.C., in 1920.

won the right to vote, so the ERA campaign did not inspire widespread enthusiasm. After the long-fought battle for the vote ended in victory, public interest in women's rights essentially vanished, and feminism went into a dormant stage for 40 years.

World War II created the need, once again, for women to take the place of men in the workplace. "Rosie the Riveter" became a symbol of society's altered structure. Even after the war, many women tried to keep their jobs, whether out of choice or financial need, but they had to face the hard fact that only men climbed to higher positions and received the highest salaries.

The feminist movement was not revived again until the 1950s. French author Simone de Beauvoir stirred international attention in 1953 with her book *The Second Sex.* In it, she described male-dominated cultures all over the world and accused men of continuing to treat women as subordinates.[17]

The Equal Rights Amendment (ERA) was passed by Congress in 1972—but failed to be ratified by the states.

In a seemingly peaceful part of the American land-
scape, a new voice emerged. Freelance journalist Betty
Friedan had graduated from Smith College with honors
in 1942, but shortly after the war she married and began
raising a family. Friedan found herself in the tidal wave
of newly affluent and middle-class Americans heading
for the suburbs.

A postwar definition of femininity was evolving, promoted primarily by women's magazines. The American
woman was discouraged from seeking a career. Working
outside the home put women in competition with men
and assertive women were considered unattractive. Instead, the ideal 1950s American woman devoted herself
to her children, kept herself attractive for her husband,
and maintained an immaculate home.

Friedan tried to be content with this lifestyle, but it became impossible for her—especially after her 15-year
class reunion at Smith College in 1957. She came away

from the campus appalled by the passivity and lack of ambition she found among her classmates. After attempting, without success, to publish articles on this disturbing topic, Friedan touched off an explosion in 1963 with the publication of her book *The Feminine Mystique*.[18]

Describing the deeply hidden discontent many homemakers felt in leading less-than-fulfilling lives, Friedan gave a powerful voice to women of her generation. She urged them to reach beyond the "comfortable concentration camp" of the home and find added fulfillment in careers. The book prompted a surge of activism unseen

Betty Friedan, *right*, and a co-worker led an early meeting of the National Organization for Women (NOW).

since the women's suffrage movement, referred to as feminism's first wave. Friedan set into motion a second wave of feminism that exerted tremendous influence over the next three decades.[19]

In 1966 Friedan helped found the National Organization for Women (NOW) to fight for equal rights for women. Friedan's NOW campaigners, with their excellent media contacts and experience as political activists and lobbyists, got dramatic results in the area of sex discrimination in the workplace.

Congress began to pass feminist-inspired legislation. The campaign for reform helped enact the Equal Pay Act of 1963 (requiring employers to pay men and women equal pay for equal work), the Civil Rights Act of 1964 (prohibiting private employers from discriminating on the basis of race, color, religion, national origin, or sex), Title IX of the Education Omnibus Act of 1972 (prohibiting sex discrimination in schools),[20] and the Equal Credit Opportunity Act (making credit more available to women), which took effect in 1975.

During the 1960s, students and other young people protested against the Vietnam War and against what they saw as a corrupt and unjust "establishment." In spite of the gains they had made, young women activists still found themselves not taken seriously or given a fair share in decision making. Many withdrew from the antiwar movement to form their own separate women's protest groups.[21]

Women's liberation became a popular topic for TV talk shows, magazines, and newspapers. In 1968 a hundred feminists picketed the Miss America pageant in Atlantic City, New Jersey, to denounce beauty contests, in which

The 1968 Miss America pageant in Atlantic City, New Jersey, drew
protests by radical feminists.

women are judged primarily by their physical qualities.
Some demonstrators threw what they viewed as symbols
of women's oppression into a trash can. Items included
girdles, false eyelashes, dishcloths, and bras. Other
demonstrators burned bras, and the negative, rather silly
image of radical feminists as bra burners still persists.[22]

Many feminist leaders, including Friedan, felt that such
demonstrations were unwise tactics. When serious campaigns for sexual equality were distorted and ridiculed,
many women were probably frightened away from the
movement. As a more ambitious and productive way to

effect change, feminists pressured the media and their advertisers to stop portraying women as sex objects or as inferior to men. At the *Washington Post,* reporters were ordered to write about female achievers with the same respect shown to males. They were warned not to describe women in physical terms such as "brunette" or "cute."[23]

The 1970s was a decade of dramatic change and progress for women. In 1972 journalist Gloria Steinem founded *Ms.* magazine, which soon became the bible of the feminist movement. In 1973 the U.S. Supreme Court's decision *Roe v. Wade* legalized abortion. The Pregnancy Discrimination Act of 1978 made it illegal for an employer to fire or demote a woman because she became pregnant.

When Ronald Reagan was elected president in 1980, feminist groups worried that many of the gains they had made would be destroyed in the name of preserving so-called traditional family values. They were right. The Reagan administration slashed budgets aimed at enforcement of sex discrimination. The administration made other cuts in such services to poor women as food stamps, school lunches, and job training programs.[24] But Reagan did make one gesture of appeasement to feminists by appointing Sandra Day O'Connor to the U.S. Supreme Court, making her the first female justice on the Court.

And the "firsts" continued. In 1983 Sally Ride became America's first female astronaut. In 1984 Walter Mondale chose Geraldine Ferraro as his running mate, making her the first female vice presidential candidate. In 1992 four new women were elected to the U.S. Senate, while in the

House of Representatives the number of women increased from 28 to 47. President Bill Clinton named a record five women to his cabinet and appointed Ruth Bader Ginsburg to the U.S. Supreme Court.

Further advances were made in the 1994 elections, even with the sweeping victories for Republicans that year. Christine Todd Whitman became the first female governor of New Jersey, for instance. Many political analysts were encouraged that she was a conservative Republican and that the public seemed to have moved beyond noticing that she was female. "That's progress," noted *Washington Times* columnist Suzanne Fields. "Whitman marks the turning point in American politics. Now women can debate the issues without also drawing attention to their sex."[25]

Perhaps the biggest feminist revolution in the years since 1970 has occurred on college campuses, where women account for 55 percent of all undergraduates; 12 percent of college and university presidents; and 39 percent of all doctorate recipients—up from 14 percent in 1970. In the early 1990s, law schools boasted student bodies that were 44 percent female, and 42 percent of all medical students were female.[26] And in the fall of 1994, the Yale School of Medicine and several other prestigious medical schools reported that women actually outnumbered men among first-year students.[27]

The decades since Betty Friedan's first book was published have seen a tremendous upheaval in the way we live. A few years ago, a bank would have refused to give a home mortgage to a single woman. In 1991, 14 percent of the homes in this country were bought or sold by women. A woman is now likely to feel comfortable

Christine Todd Whitman gave the "thumbs up" sign after she was inaugurated governor of New Jersey.

asking a man out for a movie, which represents a major shift in male-female relations. Many women still long to look like fashion models, but now women are less likely to be appreciated for their beauty than for their intelligence and talent.[28]

Even as feminists count their triumphs, however, they see more clearly than ever what still needs to be done. Friedan's groundbreaking 1963 book ended with these words, which may be just as relevant now:

> It has barely begun, the search of women for themselves. But the time is at hand when the voices of the feminine mystique can no longer drown out the inner voice that is driving women on to become complete.[29]

3
THE BACKLASH

Change does not come easily. Activists for any cause often must appear radical and somewhat "on the fringe" if they are to be effective. Some 1970s feminists held extremist views, but the majority of the voices heard during the early demonstrations were calm and rational. Unfortunately, they were seldom heard beyond their immediate (already converted) audiences. It was only when the voices got louder and more strident that they could no longer be ignored.

Conservative politicians and journalists criticized the feminist movement, and radical feminists began to come under steady attack during the 1980s. Especially troubling to the general public was the feminist campaign to alter the English language. Many of the changes were welcome and long overdue (*salesperson* instead of *salesman,* for example). Others brought ridicule—changing *history* to *herstory,* for example, or *women* to *womyn* to avoid contamination by "masculine" words. Radicals were accused of forcing rigid speech and behavioral codes on campuses and in workplaces, silencing anyone who dared to disagree with them.

During the late 1970s, Phyllis Schlafly led a STOP-ERA campaign as states considered whether to ratify the amendment.

Changes in education also took place. The achievements and importance of women had for the most part been ignored in traditional academic studies until Women's Studies became a popular major at colleges and universities nationwide. Critics of the movement, however, accused instructors of conducting group therapy rather than academic classes.

During the 1980s, many magazines and newspapers took aim at feminism with articles such as "The Feminist Mistake," or "When Feminism Failed," or "The Awful Truth about Women's Lib." The quest for women's equality was blamed for all forms of female misery, from clinical depression and homelessness to teen suicide and eating disorders.[1]

In 1986 the media seized upon an unpublished Harvard-Yale marriage study in which researchers claimed that college-educated women over 30 found it difficult to find a husband. *Newsweek* reported that a woman over 40 was "more likely to be killed by terrorists" than to get married. Reporters took statistics from this study (which were later shown to be inaccurate) and combined them with new statistics about women's infertility after age 30. Another series of articles warned about the risk of postponing marriage in favor of a career. The term *biological clock* came into common usage to warn against waiting too long for motherhood.[2]

The impact of such articles on the American public prompted a young, soft-spoken, Pulitzer-prizewinning reporter for the Wall Street Journal to investigate. Susan Faludi spent four years writing her influential book, *Backlash: The Undeclared War Against American Women,* published in 1991.

Faludi describes the backlash as a subtle but highly effective campaign against feminist goals and an attempt to roll back many of the gains made by the women's movement. Surfacing in the policies of the Reagan administration, in Hollywood, and in the mass media, the backlash was not, Faludi emphasizes, an organized conspiracy. But it succeeded in creating a distorted view of American life that caused women to question whether they really wanted equality after all. The message was that feminism is the enemy, and that too much freedom makes a woman miserable, lonely, childless, and emotionally unstable. Many movies, television shows, and advertisements featured blissful mothers, happily passive female sex objects, and frazzled career women. The "postfeminist" era had begun.[3]

Faludi's critics say that the mass media did not create or stir up female doubts and discontent. Rather, the media and entertainment industries merely reflected many women's concerns and "touch[ed] a nerve that had been rubbed raw by a generation of out-of-touch feminist leaders."[4] Other critics say Faludi's book underestimates

Susan Faludi analyzed what she called a "backlash" against American feminism.

women, treating them like weaklings who passively accept whatever the culture imposes on them.

But many American women perceived the backlash as an everyday reality, and it wasn't so much on the screen or in print as in their workplaces and homes. The backlash hit hardest in the same areas where the most progress had been made—in employment and reproduction.[5]

A History of Reversals

Backlash is nothing new. According to Faludi, each time some major headway has been made toward equality, a backlash against women's rights has occurred. American literature scholar Ann Douglas puts it this way: "The progress of women's rights in our culture, unlike other types of 'progress,' has always been strangely reversible."[6]

After Elizabeth Stanton and Susan Anthony raised their voices so strongly in Seneca Falls, for example, a counter-attack crushed women's rights appeals, warning feminists that they would end up unmarried and childless. A best-selling book in 1873 by a Harvard professor argued that women who worked suffered from infertility because of a "brain-womb" conflict.[7]

The years following ratification of the Nineteenth Amendment brought more reversals. Labor policies were enacted that protected men's jobs and denied women equal pay. After a decade of growth for female professionals, the 1920s brought their number back down. By 1930 there were fewer female doctors than in 1910. And, with the Depression of the 1930s came more federal and state laws forcing women out of the workforce.[8]

During World War II, when five to six million women flooded the workforce, the strong, independent woman became a heroic figure. In fact, the comic book character Wonder Woman was introduced in 1941. The political energies of women reintensified, and the U. S. Congress passed a record 33 bills aimed at advancing women's rights.[9]

But with the end of World War II, industry, government, and the media combined efforts to push back women's progress again. Within a year of the U.S. victory in the war, 3.25 million female workers had lost their industrial jobs. Employers complained of women having "bad attitudes" at work and of turning their backs on femininity, marriage, and motherhood. Prewar rules were again enforced against hiring married women and raising women's salaries to approach those of men's.

Faludi lamented that, "As women's collective quest for equal rights smacks into the backlash's wall of resistance, it breaks into a million pieces, each shard a separate woman's life. The backlash has ushered in not the cozy feeling of [sisterhood] . . . but the chilling realization that it is now every woman for herself."[10] Women began to feel more alone, isolated, abandoned, and powerless than ever.

In all the backlashes, women were said to be exhausted from pushing forward too fast and causing too much change too soon. But Faludi says that when women seem worn out and apathetic, it's not from making too much progress but from standing still. Whenever feminists face a strong backlash, she says, they are left "discouraged and paralyzed by the knowledge that, again, the possibility for real progress has been foreclosed."[11]

Analyzing the backlash that occurred in the 1980s, Faludi says male-female conflicts have many roots, but

Women in traditionally male jobs, such as construction work, sometimes face continuing discrimination. Susan Faludi said the traditional definition of masculinity—with husband as head of household—is partly to blame.

one of the most important is the traditional definition of masculinity. In research conducted during the last several decades, a masculine man has been identified most often and most consistently by one quality: being a good provider for his family.[12]

When recession hit in the 1980s, many jobs disappeared and wages shrank. Some men, feeling their ability to be a good breadwinner slip away, felt less secure about

In her analysis of the backlash of the 1980s, Susan Faludi said that some men felt their status as breadwinner was threatened when women began to move out of the home and into the workplace.

their masculinity. According to Faludi, this situation caused many of them to overreact and lash out at women. When a few women were promoted to management, some men claimed that "the women are taking over."

Faludi describes the early 1980s as full of "symbolic crossover points for men and women": the first time white men became less than 50 percent of the work-force, the first time more women than men enrolled in college, the first time more than 50 percent of women worked, even those with children. And 1980 was the year the U.S. Census officially stopped defining the head of household as the husband.[13]

But most of the women who took jobs during the 1980s were not stealing them from men. They were taking jobs traditionally held by women, such as clerical and service positions, most with low wages. Only a few women broke into business or management positions or into highly paid trades by becoming plumbers, carpenters, or electricians. And those who did faced discrimination that still continues. Most women cannot choose to stay home now, because they are single or because their families need two paychecks to maintain their households.[14]

A protest by disgruntled husbands showed their frustration with working wives and mothers.

The uncertain economy (and the tendency to blame women for it) may also have contributed to the rise in violence against women. Consider a few high-profile examples:

- Charles Start, a Boston fur salesman, said that he murdered his pregnant wife because she was better educated and more successful than he was, and she was gaining the "upper hand."

- Yusef Salaam, one of six men charged with raping and crushing the skull of a professional woman jogging in Central Park, told the court, he felt "like a midget, a mouse, something less than a man."

- Marc Lepine, an unemployed 25-year-old engineer, gunned down 14 women in a University of Montreal engineering classroom because they were "all a bunch of f_____ feminists."[15]

The backlash of the 1980s does not mean that feminism is dead and buried, however. Florence Howe, who founded the Feminist Press in 1970, says, "The strength of a backlash tells you how good your movement is. If you don't have a backlash, you haven't had a movement."[16]

4
The Third Wave

A resurgence of feminist, or at least female, power began to appear in the early 1990s when young feminists in their teens and twenties began calling themselves the "third wave" (the women's suffrage movement was the first, and the revolution beginning in the 1960s the second). In 1992 Yale graduate Rebecca Walker and Harvard graduate Shannon Liss founded the Third Wave Direct Action Corp [sic]. New York–based Students Organizing Students (SOS) formed in 1989 in response to the backlash against reproductive freedom. These are only two of many young activist groups forming throughout the country (mainly on college campuses, but also in high schools). They are determined to take on what members consider the unfinished work of feminism.[1]

The third wave agenda is ambitious, focusing on issues like date rape, sexual harassment, and classroom bias. Members of these diverse groups share some qualities—most notably anger and confidence. They have witnessed social change and believe they have the power to make a difference, but they also feel somewhat betrayed by second wave feminists (their mothers' generation). Third

Outside a clinic, members of Students Organizing Students (SOS) protested a gag rule—a rule barring staff from discussing abortion with clients.

wavers grew up hearing dire reports about the ravaged environment and economy they were inheriting. The AIDS epidemic exploded during their lifetime. And reports of violence against women have risen dramatically.

The third wavers' youth and rage often make their style of activism aggressive and colorful. During a 1992 protest against sexual assault at Duke University, for example, feminists staged mock attacks—ambushing men walking alone on campus and plastering them with bright pink 'Gotcha' stickers.[2]

Probably the most visible and often outrageous third wavers, however, are the "riot grrrls." This movement of young women originated in Olympia, Washington, and its founder is usually said to be Kathleen Hanna, the singer for the punk band Bikini Kill. Riot grrrls have formed an underground network of women who combine music and activism through their bands and protests. They communicate with each other through dozens of self-published pamphlets and journals, called "'zines," that are popping up around the country. The essays and poetry in the 'zines, as well as the song lyrics, openly explore female sexuality and dissatisfaction with women's roles. The riot grrrl phenomenon, Hanna says, "just shows how hungry so many women are to connect with each other."[3]

Riot grrrls are passionate and angry, but they're also hopeful. They loudly demand sexual freedom and pleasure, but they have borrowed much of the second wave's rampant suspicion of men. Bikini Kill sings, "We don't need you/Does that scare you?" And Hanna's feminist anthem, "Rebel Girl," includes these lyrics: "When she walks, the revolution's coming/In her hips, there's revolution/ When she talks, I hear the revolution/In her kiss, I taste the revolution."[4]

"Young feminists are far more courageous than we were at their age, and they have higher standards," says second wave pioneer Gloria Steinem. "In areas where I might be overly grateful for some small progress, they see vividly what is still wrong and are outraged by it."[5]

But the older, second wave feminists know how hard they've worked for even the most minor changes, and they sometimes criticize the younger generation for being spoiled and ungrateful. Criticism, however, doesn't soften the third wave approach. Nadia Moritz, director of the Young Women's Project (a group that promotes political activism), says, "We're told how much we should appreciate, for example, that we now make 70 cents to a man's dollar instead of 33. But we're not about to celebrate that."[6]

Third wavers are very aware of the second wavers' reputation for man hating, for focusing on narrow goals that didn't concern most women, and for sometimes appearing to overlook minority and low-income women. Young feminists are concerned with issues that are not exclusively feminist, such as racism, pollution, and poverty, issues that are crucial to both women and men. They welcome men into their ranks. "We want to weave our activism into the whole fabric of our lives," says Walker.[7]

Trying to attack on all fronts, third wavers think, is simply ineffective. They tend to operate in specialized arenas, choosing a focus that is important to them. It might be sex education, gay rights, or self-defense techniques. They represent such diversity that the movement has become what Friedan calls "a mosaic reflecting the new variety and complexity of women's lives."[8]

The focus is on action, though, and the results can be impressive. Walker's group registered 25,000 new voters in inner cities across the United States in 1992. SOS attracted college students across the country and launched several successful direct-action campaigns—including the boycott of the Domino's pizza chain (whose owner actively supported the antiabortion cause).

What about Men's Rights?

It is impossible to deny that feminism has permanently changed our culture. For the last three decades, men and women alike have been bombarded with feminist analyses and demands. How have men responded?

Many men have, in fact, become feminists, believing both sexes stand to gain from the feminist movement. Others have tried to ignore the challenge to change. Still others have fought back, arguing for men's rights and establishing the men's movement. Some issues of special concern to these men are affirmative action (a policy favoring previously disadvantaged groups such as women and minorities) and more fairness in child custody, child support, and visitation rights. Men have also formed hundreds of support groups, such as the National Coalition of Free Men, Men's Rights Inc., and Fathers for Equal Rights of America.

In the 1990s, the multiracial membership of SOS grew to include high school students, and it expanded its focus to include all aspects of women's physical and mental health. Its programs concentrate on training and action. Director of Programs Anna Maria Nieves says, "I want girls to view themselves as agents of change in their communities."[9]

Author Warren Farrell points out that men as well as women have been oppressed. In his book *The Myth of Male Power,* he asks why men are forced to take the dirtiest, most physically demanding and hazardous jobs; why they die earlier than women; and why they commit suicide, become alcoholic, or get heart disease, ulcers, and other stress-related diseases more often than women.[12]

A few of the groups in the men's movement focus on healing and rediscovery through emotional and spiritual retreats. Poet Robert Bly is perhaps the most well-known spokesman for this approach. Other activists emphasize listening rather than blaming. In *Fire in the Belly: On Being a Man,* author Sam Keen says healing between the sexes "will not begin until men and women cease to use their suffering as a justification for their hostility.... In the beginning we need simply to listen to each other's stories, the histories of wounds."[13]

Action can happen on a smaller scale, however, and it can involve average people, acting quietly and alone. As one young feminist put it: "Every time any woman asks for a well-deserved raise or promotion (and doesn't give up till she gets it), or calmly refuses to be bullied, she contributes to the cause."[10]

5

VOICES OF DISSENT

There are many ways to approach feminism, and no one woman or group of women can speak for all. However, second wave leaders and spokespersons remain the most recognizable modern feminists. Included among second wave feminists are such pioneers as Gloria Steinem, Germaine Greer, Susan Brownmiller, and, more recently, Susan Faludi. These and other leaders are often given much-deserved credit for the progress women have made toward equal rights since the 1960s.

Second wave activists have built a foundation upon which the future of the women's movement rests. But if they are given the credit, they are also given the blame for what is "wrong" with feminism in the 1990s.

Modern feminism may have started as a quest for equality, but by 1990, many second wave activists had narrowed their focus, zeroing in on two issues—date rape and sexual harassment. Reports of violence against women became more and more alarming, especially when they seemed to indicate that it was not *strangers* women should fear most. The image of a monster lurking in shadows gave way to an image even more ominous: the seemingly ordinary, trustworthy man who takes a woman out on a date and then rapes her. All men became suspects.

Into this atmosphere of mistrust and anger walked two people involved in what should have been a routine, barely noticed Senate hearing. President George Bush nominated Clarence Thomas for a seat on the U.S. Supreme Court, the highest court in the country. A committee of senators was ready to confirm the nomination until a woman named Anita Hill stepped forward and accused Thomas of sexually harassing her when she worked for him 10 years earlier. She faced the questions and accusations of a panel of 14 white male senators. Thomas denied the charges, and he was confirmed. Because the confirmation hearings were televised, millions of viewers witnessed the proceedings. Feminists rallied around Hill and around the complex, explosive issue of sexual harassment.

It appears, however, that the second wave's intense focus on rape and harassment has been one of the primary reasons that the feminist movement has fractured. Many activists argued that women should not depict themselves as victims, and they grew weary of sexual issues overshadowing others of equal importance, such as the economy and the environment. Sexual issues spark a sense of mistrust and miscommunication between men and women, among women, and even among feminists. During the early 1990s, many voices of dissent emerged, especially in addressing the younger generation. The voices of three women—Camille Paglia, Christina Hoff Sommers, and Katie Roiphe—stand out.

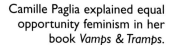

Camille Paglia explained equal opportunity feminism in her book *Vamps & Tramps*.

A "Maverick" Feminist

Camille Paglia has been called outrageous, a "maverick" feminist, a "literary pit bull," and a motormouth (because of her rapid-fire style of speaking). Paglia is a professor, an essayist, a popular speaker, and a performance artist. She charged into the public arena and instantly became notorious for her controversial views about the roles of men, women, and sex in society. Her favorite objects of attack are second wave feminists. She sees them as primarily white, economically privileged academic types, and she calls them—among other things—"thought police" and prudes.

Paglia's feminist opponents accuse her, in turn, of excusing the behavior of rapists and of blaming rape victims. Why? Because she advises young women to avoid getting drunk at fraternity parties and going with boys to their rooms. She warns that the price of sexual freedom is sexual risk, and that women must take responsibility for their own behavior.[1] Paglia is "sick of simpering white girls with their princess fantasies," and she wants a "tough-cookie feminism" that recognizes the natural power of being female.[2] She scoffs at the idea of viewing women as helpless victims and is enraged by the recent return of "nice" girls to the pedestal. She says:

> Equal opportunity feminism, which I espouse, demands the removal of all barriers to a woman's advance in the political and professional world—but not at the price of special protections for women, which are infantilizing and antidemocratic.[3]

Paglia believes second wave feminists are particularly wrong in their approach to rape and sexual harassment. She is outraged by rape, but insists that the incidence and seriousness of rape need not be exaggerated:

> What began as a useful sensitization of police officers, prosecutors, and judges to the claims of authentic rape victims turned into a hallucinatory overextension of the definition of rape to cover every unpleasant or embarrassing sexual encounter. Rape became the crime of crimes, overshadowing all the wars, massacres, and disasters of world history. The feminist obsession with rape as a symbol of male-female relations is irrational and delusional. From the perspective of the future, this period in America will look like a reign of mass psychosis, like that of the Salem witch trials.[4]

Paglia says that, in addition to distorting the issue of rape, second wave feminists have also lied to young women about sex and failed to prepare them for a world where "there never was and never will be sexual harmony."[5] Biological differences cannot be denied. She warns especially against the behavior of college men, who have just escaped the powerful domain of their mothers, are at their hormonal peak, and are struggling for a masculine identity.

What does this mean for young women? It means, among other things, that:

> Every woman must take personal responsibility for her sexuality, which is nature's red flame. She must be prudent and cautious about where she goes and with whom. When she makes a mistake, she must accept the consequences and, through self-criticism, resolve never to make that mistake again. Running to Mommy and Daddy on the campus grievance committee is unworthy of strong women. Posting lists of guilty men in the toilet is cowardly, infantile stuff.[6]

A woman's need for personal responsibility and strength also defines Paglia's view of sexual harassment. She says relying on rules and laws deprives women of their freedom from authority figures. Women should rely on themselves and take charge of the situation, according to Paglia. When confronted by a harasser, she says simply, "Deal with it. On the spot." Tell the jerk to stop. Women with this kind of take-charge attitude, Paglia says, will be harassed less often.[7]

Crusader against Distortion

When a previously unknown philosophy professor at Clark University wrote the book *Who Stole Feminism* in 1994, she was not surprised by the controversy it stirred. Christina Hoff Sommers had, after all, taken on some of the most powerful leaders of modern feminism. She hasn't exactly endeared herself to other women with statements such as this:"There are a lot of homely women in women's studies. Preaching these antimale, antisex sermons is a way for them to compensate for various heartaches—they're just mad at the beautiful girls."[8]

As the reviewer in *Time* magazine put it, the point of Sommers's book is that "feminism has been derailed by a bunch of neurotic, self-indulgent intellectuals who have a direct personal interest in grossly overstating the woes of womankind."[9] Sommers considers herself a feminist, but she gradually became appalled by what she saw happening to young college women, especially those who took women's studies classes. She claimed that many female students changed dramatically during their freshman year, becoming sullen converts to the radical feminist belief that they were horribly oppressed by men and by society.

She wrote her book because she did not like what the feminist movement had become. Sommers divides the

Christina Hoff Sommers cautioned feminists against exaggerating the difficulties of women.

movement into equity feminists and gender feminists. Equity feminists point with pride to the gains women have achieved, particularly in the area of legal reforms, which used to be the focus of second wave feminism. Gender feminists, by contrast, say such progress is an illusion, and that American women are "not the free creatures we think we are."[10] Gender feminists describe American society as a patriarchy that keeps women frightened and submissive. Sommers writes:

> The feminists who hold this divisive view of our social and political reality believe that all our institutions, from the state to the family to the grade schools, perpetuate

Some young women on college campuses come to believe they are oppressed—a belief Christine Sommers challenges.

male dominance. Believing that women are virtually under siege, the "gender feminists" naturally seek recruits to their side of the gender war. They seek support. They seek vindication. They seek ammunition.[11]

Gender feminists most often find recruits on college campuses. Sommers spoke to several young women who told her about their own personal transformations and how their view of the world was suddenly altered by the radical feminist perspective. Laurie, a women's studies graduate from Vassar, told Sommers, "You're never the same again. You become so aware of things."[12]

Anne, a University of Pennsylvania student, related how students called this keen new awareness "being on the verge" or "bottoming out." "You are down on everything. Nothing is funny anymore. You hit rock bottom and ask: how can I live my life?" When Sommers suggested to this well-educated, privileged young woman that to others she might appear quite fortunate, Anne continued to speak of suffering and psychological oppression: "If you feel like the whole world is on top of you, then it is."[13]

How are such "conversions" achieved? Is it just a matter of peer pressure? According to Sommers, one method of persuasion is to create and perpetuate myths about how downtrodden American women really are. Feminist research is often used to rally others to their cause by distorting or exaggerating the facts. It is almost always possible to "prove" something in a study if that's the purpose of the study. And even when feminists use more objective research, Sommers has found that many errors have been made, or statistics misinterpreted, whether deliberately or not. If hyped enough by the media, then these distortions become accepted as hard facts in the eyes of the American public.

Sommers offered several examples. Perhaps the most well known is the Super Bowl hoax of January 1993. At a news conference, a coalition of women's groups told reporters that Super Bowl Sunday was "the biggest day of the year for violence against women." Studies supposedly showed that 40 percent more women would be battered on that day. Meanwhile, these groups had sent mailings to at-risk women, warning them not to stay home during the game. Journalists picked up the story and reported this "fact" widely. The *New York Times* dubbed the game the "Abuse Bowl," and CBS labeled Super Bowl Sunday a day of dread. Within a few days, the authors of the study denied finding any relation between football and domestic violence. The story proved to be false, but the Super Bowl "statistic" remains in the public realm.[14]

Sommers unmasked several other embarrassing exaggerations and mistakes in feminist literature. Naomi Wolf, in her widely quoted book *The Beauty Myth,* mistakenly claimed that 150,000 women die in a "holocaust" of anorexia every year (a situation Wolf blamed more on men than on the women themselves). But Wolf confused the number of *sufferers* with the number of *deaths.*[15] Feminists claimed that the battering of pregnant women was the number one cause of birth defects in America; the March of Dimes, to whom this widely cited statistic was attributed, denied any knowledge of it.[16] Sommers pointed out other exaggerations in the number of campus rapes, and wife beatings, and in accounts of how girls are discriminated against in the classroom.

When even a single case of rape or battering or one example of sex discrimination in schools is cause enough for alarm, why do some feminists overstate the problems? Sommers said that inflated numbers "serve a political agenda." Assault and rape become more than isolated acts of individual men; they are instead seen as within the normal range of male behavior and part of "men's undeclared war on women."[17]

As a woman who believes that much remains to be done for the women of the world, and who sees a crucial role for feminism, Sommers is concerned about the future of the movement. The new crop of young, radical feminists seems "even angrier, more resentful, and more indifferent to the truth than their mentors." Since the majority of women are not so enraged or convinced of their own oppression by men, they are distancing themselves from the feminist movement.[18] She writes:

I do not mean to confuse the women who work in the trenches to help the victims of true abuse and discrimination with the gender feminists whose falsehoods and exaggerations are muddying the waters of American feminism. These feminist ideologues are helping no one; on the contrary, their divisive and resentful philosophy adds to the woes of our society and hurts legitimate feminism.[19]

An Antifeminist Backlasher?
Katie Roiphe is often called a traitor, an antifeminist, a backlasher, even a female Clarence Thomas. For expressing her ideas, she has received threats. But Katie Roiphe does consider herself a feminist.

In 1993, when she was only 25 years old, this Princeton graduate student published a book that was one of the most applauded—and most criticized—books about feminism to come along in decades. Entitled *The Morning After: Sex, Fear, and Feminism on Campus,* Roiphe's book describes her firsthand experiences with the hysteria that has gripped college campuses. Thanks to the "rape culture" allegedly created by second wave feminists, Roiphe says an image has emerged of women as victims who are harassed by a professor's sexist joke and who give in to verbal pressure to have sex and then later call it rape.[20]

In her book, Roiphe, like Paglia, examines what she believes to be the two primary focuses of feminists—rape and sexual harassment. The result of that focus has been a rigid political correctness within the feminist movement. Roiphe wrote the book in response to the political climate she found on college campuses, the feeling of *us* against *them,* and the expectation that students not stray from the current feminist belief system and language.[21] She writes:

> At Harvard, and later at graduate school in English literature at Princeton, I was surprised at how many things there were not to say, at the arguments and assertions that could not be made, lines that could not be crossed, taboos that could not be broken. . . . Listening to feminist conversations, in and out of class, I was surprised at how fenced in they were, how little territory there was that could actually be disputed.[22]

Roiphe says that what shapes campus feminism is the current sexual climate—an intense fear of being raped and of getting AIDS. Young women find themselves bombarded with warnings about sexual relationships. According to Roiphe, this climate is what causes thousands

The Women's Action Coalition led a protest against rape—a key concern of third wave feminists.

of women across the country to protest annually against sexual violence in what are known as Take Back the Night marches:

> Take Back the Night offers tangible targets, things to chant against and rally around in a sexually ambiguous time. Take Back the Night is a symptom of conservative attitudes about sex mingling with the remains of the sexual revolution. The crisis is not a rape crisis, but a crisis in sexual identity.[23]

Katie Roiphe warned women against seeing themselves as victims.

Not all Take Back the Night protests are identical, and in many communities the concern is with all crime, not just rape. But Roiphe calls the various protests she has witnessed "march as therapy," in which many women (and a few men) get up in front of the crowds to relate their own stories of rape, assault, and incest.[24] The rest of the participants listen, cry, hold hands, light candles, and chant. Roiphe finds all this a disturbing substitute for religion.[25] The atmosphere is one of mass confession. She writes, "I find the public demand—and it is a demand—for intimacy strange and unconvincing. Public confidences have a peculiarly aggressive quality."[26] Most of the speakers are sincere, but some women have exaggerated or even fabricated stories in order to participate and get attention.

The most consistent theme in the "speak-outs" is the need to break the silence, a theme which Roiphe finds ironic:

> These Princeton women, future lawyers, newspaper reporters, investment bankers, are hardly the voiceless, by most people's definition. But silence is poetic. Being silenced is even more poetic. These days people vie for the position of being silenced, but being silenced is necessarily a construction of the articulate. Once you're talking about being voiceless, you're already talking. The first Take Back the Night march at Princeton was more than 10 years ago, and every year they're breaking the silence all over again. The fashionable cloak of silence is more about style than content. Built into the rhetoric about silence is the image of a malign force clamping its hands over the mouths of victims.[27]

While these marches are intended to celebrate women's strength, Roiphe believes that instead they celebrate women's vulnerability. She says, "This is a dead-end gesture. Proclaiming victimhood doesn't help project strength."[28] Roiphe does not deny that violent crime is a problem, but she feels *everyone* is at risk. "Fear is not exclusively feminine."[29]

Roiphe does not blame radical feminists alone for the rape crisis. Beginning in the mid-1980s, the media sharply raised public interest in rape with several alarming revelations. The results of a study of campus rape published in 1985 by *Ms.* magazine became widely quoted: one in four college women is the victim of rape or attempted rape.[30] The problem, for Roiphe and many others, is that these results are strongly influenced by the definition of rape.

Everyone agrees that being attacked and raped by a stranger is horrifying. But what about a woman who is verbally coaxed into sex by a date? Or when she has sex under the influence of alcohol or drugs? Or when she later recognizes a sexual act as rape? When the word is used to describe anything with sexual content that is unpleasant or uncertain between a man and a woman, the term becomes meaningless either as description or accusation. And it can serve to trivialize real rape:

> Whether or not one in four college women has been raped, then, is a matter of opinion, not a matter of mathematical fact. . . . There is a gray area in which someone's rape may be another person's bad night.[31]

Not only have many students come to believe that one-in-four statistic, they think it's low—that probably more like half of all women have experienced this form of violence. To Roiphe, "This is the true crisis: that there are a not insignificant number of young women walking around with this alarming belief."[32]

Like date rape, sexual harassment has become a feminist battle cry. There is no doubt that sexual harassment occurs. Some students are forced into sex in exchange for good grades, for example, and some women (and men) face being fired or demoted if they say "no" to an employer. But Roiphe claims that the term is not always used to describe *extreme* behavior. Sometimes "sexual harassment" looks much like common everyday experiences. Suddenly everything between men and women comes under suspicion and scrutiny. And you may not realize you are a "survivor" of sexual harassment until it is pointed out to you by feminists.

Because of this obsession with victimization, Roiphe warns that "To create awareness is sometimes to create a problem."[33] She continues:

> The word "uncomfortable" echoes through all the litera-
> ture on sexual harassment. The feminists concerned with
> this issue, then, propose the right to be comfortable as a
> feminist principle. The difficulty with these rules is that,
> although it may infringe on the right to comfort, unwant-
> ed sexual attention is part of nature. To find wanted sexu-
> al attention, you have to give and receive a certain amount
> of unwanted sexual attention. Clearly, the truth is that if
> no one was ever allowed to risk offering unsolicited sex-
> ual attention, we would all be solitary creatures.[34]

On college campuses, all the warnings against and fear of male professors may reduce the number of abusive connections they make with students, but it is also certain to reduce the number of helpful connections.[35]

Since sexual harassment is usually seen as an abuse of power, Roiphe particularly objects to those claims against men who have equal—or even less—power than the female "victim." Why, she asks, are women seeing their authority as so fragile that it crumbles automatically in the presence of males?[36]

There must be a better way for women and men to relate to each other.

6
POWER FEMINISM

Second wave feminists are often accused of downplaying gender differences and, in effect, arguing that men and women are virtually the same. It is difficult to push for equality in the eyes of the law and society and at the same time admit that men and women are different in significant ways. Women fought hard and long against discrimination based on hormonal issues, for example—arguing that menstrual periods, maternal instincts, and PMS (premenstrual syndrome) do not make women less able to do their jobs than men. Do women dare acknowledge that hormones, or anything else, make them different? Does difference have to mean worse or better?

Recent scientific research seems to indicate that gender differences (in addition to hormonal ones) do exist, and they are not all learned or forced on us by society. Many differences appear at birth. Several studies of babies and toddlers seem to show that boys and girls respond in distinctly different ways to their environment. Many feminists continue to claim that we raise our boys differently from girls, and that's why, for example, boys play with guns and trucks and girls play with dolls and makeup.

But it is difficult to ignore scientific research such as

that of neuropsychologist Ruben C. Gur. In 1995, he published his finding that the brains of men and women are identical except in the region that deals with emotional response. Because of this difference in the brain, he argued, the emotions that cause a man to fight are likely to cause a woman to talk or cry.[1]

Not all feminists, however, argue against gender differences. Many celebrate them. In 1982 psychologist Carol Gilligan published an intriguing and influential book, *In a Different Voice,* and became one of the primary voices for "difference feminism." This branch of the movement paid tribute to women's nurturing and relationship skills and their "ethic of caring." Difference feminists point to what they see as natural (as well as cultural) differences between males and females in order to explain why so little criminal violence is committed by women. Gender differences explain why women dominate in "caring professions" such as nursing and social work and why women are much less likely than men to abandon their children.

This view became very popular during the 1980s, as feminist Katha Pollitt observed in *The Nation:*

> By arguing that the traditional qualities, tasks, and ways of life of women are as important, valuable, and serious as those of men (if not more so), Gilligan and others let women feel that nothing needs to change except the social valuation accorded to what they are already doing. It's a rationale for the status quo, which is why men like it, and it's a burst of grateful applause for womanhood, which is why women like it. Men keep the power, but since power is bad, so much the worse for them.[2]

Katha Pollitt wasn't the only feminist to examine the popularity of difference feminism as the 1990s began.

According to the feminist author Naomi Wolf, difference feminism "created a world view which said that men were responsible for all evil and women are all angels of light. That increasingly polarizes the genders."[3] Furthermore, she points out that seeking equality sometimes requires women to give up advantages.

> I know scores of women—independent, autonomous— who avoid assuming any of the risk for a romantic or sexual approach. I have watched strong women stand by while their partners wrestle with a stuck window, an intractable computer printer, maps, and locks. But people are lazy—yes, even women sometimes—and it's easy to rationalize that the person with the penis is the one who should get out of a warm bed to fix the snow on the TV screen. After all, it's the very least owed to us in compensation for centuries of enslavement. But passivity isn't equality.[4]

Polarizing the genders has had other effects as well. It has led some feminists to an obsession with victimization. Wolf is one of the most eloquent spokespersons against emphasizing women as victims. She favors what she calls "power feminism." Author of *The Beauty Myth* (1989) and *Fire with Fire* (1994), Wolf was already being proclaimed the new Gloria Steinem before she was 33 years old. But she considers herself part of the "third wave" of American feminism.

Wolf says that the gains in power made by women in the 1970s were eroded so badly under Ronald Reagan's presidency that a feminism based on gaining rights gave way to "feminism of compassion." According to Wolf, "Women could no longer get a reaction by saying 'this isn't fair, we're human beings.' They had to say 'have pity on us, we're hurt.'" And too often women were "trapped in a psychology in which we think if we are 'nice' girls for long enough and keep whining, 'they' will see it's not fair and 'they' will make it better."[5]

Feminists who focus on victimization, according to Wolf, "make heroes" of women who have committed violent, vindictive crimes, such as Lorena Bobbitt (who cut off her abusive husband's penis and then was acquitted in court). Wolf and many other analysts of the infamous Bobbitt case found it odd that because Lorena was a victim, whatever she did was justified. Many feminists nationwide were hailing the symbolic importance of this

Lorena Bobbitt mutilated her abusive husband—and won sympathy from some people.

mutilation. But Wolf says, "Victimization does not equal
innocent and good."[6]

Whenever someone is victimized, an imbalance of
power exists. Wolf says that the balance of power has
changed dramatically since the backlash years. And she
points to a single monumental event as the turning
point—the 1991 Senate confirmation hearings of
Clarence Thomas.

Anita Hill's testimony against Thomas, accusing him of
sexual harassment, "set in motion a train of events that
led American women into becoming the political ruling
class—probably the only ruling class ever to be unaware
of its status."[7] This event further divided men and
women and caused what Wolf calls a "genderquake"—a

Anita Hill came forward
to testify against Clarence
Thomas, *opposite,* when
he was nominated to the
Supreme Court.

shift that brought about unprecedented female political activism and power. She says that the theme of the 1992 elections (at local, state, and national levels) was retaliation. Record numbers of women ran for office, many of them out of anger about the Thomas-Hill hearings. In addition, polls during the campaign showed President George Bush scoring far lower with women than with men; Wolf believes that the failure of Republican leaders to listen to the women in their party probably cost them the White House.[8]

Gains for women in the early 1990s included such legislative triumphs as the Family Leave Act and several antistalking bills. The budget for research on breast cancer and other women's health problems doubled. And

President Clinton appointed several women to cabinet posts and another—Ruth Bader Ginsberg—to the Supreme Court. In addition, much of the previous decade's antiabortion legislation was reversed.[9] The events of 1992, political and cultural shifts, show that:

> When women voice their opinions, it works. Obviously, women's groups have been saying this for years. But women as a whole must see from the genderquake that the conditions of our lives can be drastically changed for the better when we do that simple thing so contrary to female socialization: believe that our opinions count.[10]

Equality may well be within women's grasp, but Wolf fears that they may back away from it, "clinging to an outdated image of ourselves as powerless, [and] inch along for another hundred years or so, subject to the whims and wind shifts of whatever form of backlash comes along next."[11]

Why should power feminism be so difficult to translate into everyday life? One reason has historical as well as psychological roots. Wolf writes:

> Women's lives are changing at the speed of light compared with the lives of their mothers and grandmothers. The embrace of power is behavior that would have had women burned at the stake not too long ago. The psychology of the separate sphere feels like home. So at a time when many women are actually learning to use power, a threat is posed to our psychological comfort. In response, victim feminism took the better-worn path backward, rather than forging ahead.[12]

And, of course, women are not alone in their resistance to change. "Men are not being asked to 'share'

Supreme Court Justice
Ruth Bader Ginsberg was
nominated to the Court
by President Bill Clinton.

power, the way, in a good marriage, they are being asked
to 'share' the housework. They are being forcefully
pressed to yield power,"[13] Wolf says. Many feminists see
sexism as evidence that men want to "oppress" women.
While this may be true for some misogynists (women-
haters), most men are simply trying desperately, and naturally, to hang on to what they have. Wolf says that women
have to understand the nature of power, and their own

Naomi Wolf said power feminists have "no difficulty telling the difference between hating sexism and hating men."

will to have it. She believes that if the roles had been reversed—if women had been in power throughout history—*they* would be the sexist ones, resistant to *men's* equality.[14]

It's not difficult to understand men's desperation to retain power when you consider that, during the 1970s and 1980s, women began to invade the cultural and political domains of men. Women became construction workers, executives, college presidents, and soldiers. Female athletes gained on male records and female theologians began to question whether or not God is male.[15]

In addition, male authority was eroded by the fact that more and more women and children came forward to reveal what men had done to them. Wolf wrote that thanks to studies showing "the staggering frequency with which many men beat and rape their wives and girlfriends, and sexually assault children, the myth evaporated that such behavior was that exceptional."[16]

Wolf celebrates this change in attitude along with all the other gains for women. But she is quick to point out the enormous burdens that remain: "Subsidized child care is a rarity; most women have been sexually harassed at work; the court system is almost useless in deterring rape and domestic violence; and women are paid less than men for doing the same jobs."[17]

The question Wolf asks is "not whether society is ready to yield to women their rightful places, but whether women themselves are ready to take possession of them."[18] And her solution lies in power feminism.

> [Power feminism] means taking practical giant steps instead of ideologically pure baby steps; practicing tolerance rather than self-righteousness. Power feminism encourages us to identify with one another primarily through the shared pleasures and strengths of femaleness, rather than primarily through our shared vulnerability and pain. It calls for alliances based on economic self-interest and economic giving back rather than on a sentimental and workable fantasy of cosmic sisterhood.[19]

A power feminist "has no difficulty telling the difference between hating sexism and hating men."[20] Sexism clearly does exist, and many men do need to hold themselves accountable for it, but declaring that the male population is innately sexist or violent or anything else is man bashing. And that "is a reflex grossly unworthy of feminism, which should be the ultimate human-rights movement."[21]

Wolf sees the feminist movement warmly embracing all individuals regardless of gender, race, religion, income, education, or sexual orientation. She calls for diversity in attitudes toward abortion and other women's issues that used to call for an automatic, prescribed feminist response. And she certainly sees an active role for politically conservative women.[22]

Wolf openly disagrees with much of what dissidents like Paglia and Roiphe have to say. But to Wolf, dissent is not dangerous. She says not all feminists automatically dread new ideas; many do, however, fear the backlash legislation that may result from such dissent:

> When some feminists resist Camille Paglia's wide opinion that women who go to a man's room are asking for date rape, or a Katie Roiphe's view that the "rape crisis" is imaginary, it is because such language can elicit not only a fun debate, but also an actual rollback of women's legal rights.[23]

What does power feminism in action look like? Wolf says that, to begin with, power feminists assume that women can gather together their power and that they can win. They recognize where the system works unfairly, and then proceed to "use their resources to force it to change, rather than pleading for kinder treatment on the basis of one's victim status."[24]

One way to marshal women's power, Wolf says, is in the formation of "power groups." These are similar to women's support groups from the past, but rather than emphasizing sisterhood, consciousness-raising, and the sharing of negative memories and emotions, the power group aims at practical results. Women are asked not to share their stories so much as to recount their individual skills and resources. Since money is always necessary for activism—and women usually lack it—they are taught how to raise funds and use them efficiently. Even more importantly, they share the most valuable asset in today's economy: information.[25]

One of the many success stories of power feminism is that of the Take Our Daughters to Work Day. In April 1993, the Ms. Foundation sponsored this day to take girls into their parents' workplaces and instill in them the ambition and self-esteem to help them succeed. The day was—and continues to be—a huge success. With a million parents participating, the event attracts very positive media coverage.

This mother shared an afternoon with her daughter during Take Our Daughters to Work Day.

In *Fire with Fire,* Naomi Wolf writes:

The day was a perfect example of flexible power feminism. It positioned no one as a victim. It appealed to Republicans and Democrats, the religious and the secular, men and women, urban and rural. Self-confidence is a unit of potential power for each woman to translate into her own goals, and young girls are, themselves, units of potential power.[26]

Among Wolf's other strategies for power feminists:

• Avoid generalizations about men that imply that their maleness is the unchangeable source of the problem.

• Never judge men in a way that we would consider sexist if men applied it to women.

• Resist the notion that there are any fixed truths or right answers about feminism.

• Institute "Power 101" courses in high schools so girls of all backgrounds know how to debate, fund-raise, call a press conference, run a campaign, read contracts, negotiate leases and salaries, and manage a financial portfolio.[27]

Wolf concludes that "we have reached a moment at which sexual inequality, which we think of as being the texture and taste of femininity itself, can begin to become a quaint memory of the old country—if we are not too attached to it to let it go."[28]

The Future of Feminism

It should be clear by now that feminism plays an essential —if troubled—role in American society. Warnings of its demise are as old as the movement itself. What seems to be important as the 20th century draws to a close, however, is that feminism, like every aspect of our culture, needs to celebrate diversity, not fear or suppress it. And young men and women will find their own style, their own way to be together at school, in the streets, at work and at home. People grow and change with time; so do political and cultural movements . . . like feminism.

If we turn to two of the most prominent feminists in history, Gloria Steinem and Betty Friedan, perhaps they can provide some clarity for the future:

> It's a big leap to think that what happens to you every day—in the secretarial pool, at the shopping center—has anything to do with who is in the Senate or the White House. The connection is just beginning to be forged. We are only 25 years into what by all precedent is a century of feminism. But once you get a majority consciousness change, you also get a backlash. It's both an inevitable tribute to success and a danger. The future depends entirely on what each of us does every day. After all, a movement is only people moving.[29]

> Gloria Steinem

> Young women are the true daughters of feminism; they take nothing for granted and are advancing the cause with marvelous verve. If they keep doing what they're doing, 30 years from today we may not need a feminist movement. We may have achieved real equality.[30]

> Betty Friedan

Endnotes

Chapter 1. Fear of Feminism

[1] Tracy Tullis, "Feminists Under Fire," Minneapolis *Star Tribune,* February 28, 1994.

[2] Nancy Gibbs, "The War Against Feminism," *Time,* March 9, 1992, 51.

[3] Katie Roiphe, *The Morning After: Sex, Fear, and Feminism on Campus* (New York: Little, Brown & Company, 1993), 3.

[4] Joannie M. Schrof, "Feminism's Daughters," *U.S. News & World Report,* September 27, 1993, 70.

[5] Susan D. Haas, "Feminists Are Victims of Today's Witch-Hunt," Minneapolis *Star Tribune,* November 2, 1993.

[6] Gibbs, 54.

[7] Editors, "Let's Get Real about Feminism: the Backlash, the Myths, the Movement," *Ms.,* September/October 1993, 35.

[8] Ibid., 43.

[9] Lisa Maria Hogeland, "Fear of Feminism," *Ms.,* November/December 1994, 20.

[10] Naomi Wolf, *Fire with Fire: The New Female Power and How It Will Change the 21st Century* (New York: Random House, 1993), 77.

[11] Elizabeth Fox-Genovese, *Feminism without Illusions* (Chapel Hill N.C.: The University of North Carolina Press, 1991), 2.

[12] Hogeland, 20.

[13] Susan Faludi, *Backlash: The Undeclared War Against American Women* (New York: Crown Publishers, Inc., 1991), 58.

[14] Gibbs, 54.

[15] Laura Shapiro, "Why Women Are Angry," *Newsweek,* October 21, 1991, 44.

[16] Peter T. Kilborn, "Top Corporate Jobs Still Elude Most Minorities, Women," Minneapolis *Star Tribune,* March 16, 1995.

[17] Alva Benn, "What We're Still Fighting For," *Cosmopolitan*, May 1994, 201.

[18] Editors, "The Many Faces of Feminism," *Ms.*, July/August 1994, 33.

Chapter 2. The First 150 Years

[1] Susan Alice Watkins, Marisa Rueda and Marta Rodriquez, *Introducing Feminism* (Cambridge, England: Icon Books Ltd., 1994), 4.

[2] Ibid., 14.

[3] Jules Archer, *Breaking Barriers* (New York: Viking, 1991), 3.

[4] Watkins et al., 17.

[5] Also named Mary, her daughter grew up to marry the Romantic poet Percy Bysshe Shelley. Mary Shelley is the author of the classic science-fiction novel *Frankenstein*.

[6] Archer, 4.

[7] Ibid.

[8] Ibid., 5.

[9] Christina Hoff Sommers, *Who Stole Feminism?* (New York: Simon & Schuster, 1994), 35.

[10] Archer, 7.

[11] Ibid., 6.

[12] Watkins et al., 45.

[13] Clark Morphew, "Spiritualists led way to women's rights," *St. Paul Pioneer Press*, November 19, 1994, 9D.

[14] Faludi, xxiii.

[15] Archer, 10.

[16] Ibid., 11.

[17] Ibid.

[18] David Halberstam, "The Unhappy Housewife," *St. Paul Pioneer Press*, July 6, 1993.

[19] Joannie M. Schrof, "Feminism's Daughters," *U.S. News & World Report,* September 27, 1993, 68.

[20] Archer, 12.

[21] Ibid., 13.

[22] Watkins et al., 105

[23] Archer, 14.

[24] Ibid., 167.

[25] Suzanne Fields, "Whitman rightly debates issues without playing the gender card," *St. Paul Pioneer Press,* February 3, 1995.

[26] Andrea Peyser, "Gains—We've Come a Long Way, Baby!" *Cosmopolitan,* May 1994, 198.

[27] "Women start outnumbering men at nation's top medical schools," Minneapolis *Star Tribune,* May 31, 1995.

[28] Peyser, 198.

[29] Betty Friedan, *It Changed My Life: Writings on the Women's Movement* (New York: Dell Publishing, 1977), 14.

Chapter 3. The Backlash

[1] Faludi, xi.

[2] Gibbs, 52.

[3] Ibid., 51.

[4] Ibid.

[5] Faludi, 55.

[6] Ibid., 46.

[7] Ibid., 49.

[8] Ibid., 50.

[9] Ibid., 51.

[10] Ibid., 58.

[11] Ibid.

[12] Ibid., 65.

[13] Ibid., 67.

[14] Shapiro, 43.

[15] Faludi, 67.

[16] Shapiro, 43.

Chapter 4. The Third Wave

[1] Schrof, 69.

[2] Ibid.

[3] Editors, *Ms.*, July/August 1994, 60.

[4] Ibid.

[5] Schrof, 69.

[6] Ibid., 70.

[7] Ibid., 71.

[8] Ibid.

[9] Editors, *Ms.*, July/August 1994, 35.

[10] Diane Baroni, "Feminist . . . What Is It about That Word?" *Cosmopolitan,* May 1994, 197.

[11] Cathy Young, "Hey, We Can Be Victims Too," Minneapolis *Star Tribune,* January 24, 1995.

[12] Lance Morrow, "Men: Are They Really That Bad?" *Time,* February 14, 1994, 56.

[13] Sam Keen, "The Blame Game," *Utne Reader,* January/February 1993, 68.

Chapter 5. Voices of Dissent

[1] Wendy Kaminer, "Feminism's Identity Crisis," *The Atlantic Monthly,* October 1993, 68.

[2] Camille Paglia, *Vamps & Tramps* (New York: Vintage Books, 1994), xii.

[3] Ibid., x.

[4] Ibid., 24.

[5] Ibid., 65.

[6] Camille Paglia, "It's a Jungle Out There, So Get Used to It!" *Utne Reader,* January/February 1993, 65.

[7] Ibid.

[8] Tad Friend, "Goddess, riot grrrl, philosopher-queen, lipstick lesbian, warrior, tattooed love child, sack artist, leader of men," *Esquire,* February 1994, 55.

[9] Barbara Ehrenreich, "A Feminist on the Outs," *Time,* August 1, 1994, 61.

[10] Christina Hoff Sommers, "Figuring Out Feminism," *National Review,* June 27, 1994, 32.

[11] Ibid.

[12] Sommers, *Who Stole Feminism?* 47.

[13] Ibid.

[14] Sommers, "Figuring Out Feminism," 33.

[15] Ibid., 30.

[16] Ibid., 32.

[17] Ian Maitland, "Feminists' misuse of statistics is grossly unfair to both sexes," Minneapolis *Star Tribune,* August 8, 1994.

[18] Sommers, *Who Stole Feminism,* 18.

[19] Ibid., 17.

[20] Sarah Crichton, "Sexual Correctness: Has it Gone Too Far?" *Newsweek,* October 25, 1993, 52.

[21] Kris Worrell, "Young author strikes nerve in critique of feminism's 'rape culture,'" *St. Paul Pioneer Press,* October 5, 1993.

[22] Roiphe, 5.

[23] Ibid., 26.

[24] Ibid., 37.

[25] Ibid., 38.

[26] Ibid., 43.

[27] Ibid., 34.

[28] Ibid., 44.

[29] Ibid., 47.

[30] Ibid., 51.

[31] Ibid., 54.

[32] Ibid., 58.

[33] Ibid., 110.

[34] Ibid., 87.

[35] Ibid., 95.

[36] Ibid., 90.

Chapter 6. Power Feminism

[1] "Gender Lines of Emotion," *Star Tribune,* January 27, 1995.

[2] Katha Pollitt, "Are Women Morally Superior to Men?" *Utne Reader,* September/October 1993, 101.

[3] Mary Ann Grossman, "Power Feminism," *St. Paul Pioneer Press,* December 13, 1993.

[4] Naomi Wolf, "Can You Be a Feminist and Love Men Too?" *Cosmopolitan,* May 1994, 202.

[5] Karin Winegar, "Naomi Wolf says the time is ripe for 'power feminism,'" *Star Tribune,* January 3, 1994.

[6] Grossman, 2C.

[7] Naomi Wolf, *Fire with Fire,* xv.

[8] Ibid., 7.

[9] Ibid., 26.

[10] Ibid., 34.

[11] Ibid., xv.

[12] Ibid., 177.

[13] Ibid., 12.

[14] Ibid., 14.

[15] Ibid., 17.

[16] Ibid., 18.

[17] Ibid., 51.

[18] Ibid., 52.

[19] Ibid., 53.

[20] Ibid.

[21] Ibid., 151.

[22] Ibid., 60.

[23] Ibid., 108.

[24] Ibid., 166.

[25] Ibid., 300.

[26] Ibid., 306.

[27] Ibid., 316.

[28] Ibid., 320.

[29] Nancy Gibbs and Jeanne McDowell, "How to Revive a Revolution," *Time,* March 9, 1992, 57.

[30] Schrof, 71.

Resources

Equal Employment Advisory Council
1015 15th Street NW
Suite 1220
Washington, DC 20005
202-789-8650

Equal Employment Opportunity Commission (EEOC)
1801 L Street NW
Washington, DC 20507
202-663-4264 or
800-669-EEOC

Equal Rights Advocates
1663 Mission Street
Suite 550
San Francisco, CA 94103
415-621-0672

Ms. Foundation for Women
141 Fifth Avenue
Suite 6-S
New York, NY 10010
212-353-8580

9to5
National Association of
Working Women
614 Superior Avenue
NW, Room 852
Cleveland, OH 44113
216-566-9308 or
800-522-0925

National Organization for Women (NOW)
1000 16th Street NW
Suite 700
Washington, DC 20036
202-331-0066

National Woman's Party
144 Constitution
Avenue NE
Washington, DC 20002
202-546-1210

Women's Action Alliance
370 Lexington Avenue
Suite 603
New York, NY 10017
212-532-8330

Bibliography

Archer, Jules. *Breaking Barriers.* New York: Viking, 1991.

Baroni, Diane. "Feminist . . . What Is It about That Word?" *Cosmopolitan,* May 1994, 196-197.

Benn, Alva. "What We're Still Fighting For." *Cosmopolitan,* May 1994, 200-201.

Crichton, Sarah. "Sexual Correctness: Has It Gone Too Far?" *Newsweek,* October 25, 1993, 52-56.

Editors. "The Many Faces of Feminism." *Ms.,* July/August 1994, 33-63.

_____. "Let's Get Real about Feminism: the Backlash, the Myths, the Movement." *Ms.,* September/October 1993, 34-43.

Ehrenreich, Barbara. "A Feminist on the Outs." *Time,* August 1, 1994, 61.

Faludi, Susan. *Backlash: The Undeclared War against American Women.* New York: Crown Publishers, Inc., 1991.

Fox-Genovese, Elizabeth. *Feminism without Illusions.* Chapel Hill, N. C.: The University of North Carolina Press, 1991.

Friend, Tad. "Goddess, riot grrrl, philosopher-queen, lipstick lesbian, warrior, tattooed love child, sack artist, leader of men." *Esquire,* February 1994, 47-55.

Friedan, Betty. *It Changed My Life: Writings on the Women's Movement.* New York: Dell Publishing, 1977.

Gibbs, Nancy. "The War Against Feminism." *Time,* March 9, 1992, 50-55.

Gibbs, Nancy, and Jeanne McDowell. "How to Revive a Revolution." *Time,* March 9, 1992, 56-57.

Hogeland, Lisa Maria. "Fear of Feminism." *Ms.,* November/December 1994, 18-21.

Kaminer, Wendy. "Feminism's Identity Crisis." *The Atlantic Monthly,* October 1993, 51-68.

Keen, Sam. "The Blame Game." *Utne Reader,* January/February 1993, 65-68.

Morrow, Lance. "Men: Are They Really That Bad?" *Time,* February 14, 1994, 53-59.

Paglia, Camille. *Vamps & Tramps.* New York: Vintage Books, 1994.

_____. "It's a Jungle Out There, So Get Used to It!" *Utne Reader,* January/February 1993, 61-65.

Peyser, Andrea. "Gains—We've Come a Long Way, Baby!" *Cosmopolitan,* May 1994, 198-199.

Pollitt, Katha. "Are Women Morally Superior to Men?" *Utne Reader,* September/October 1993, 101-109.

Roiphe, Katie. *The Morning After: Sex, Fear, and Feminism on Campus.* New York: Little, Brown & Company, 1993.

Schrof, Joannie M. "Feminism's Daughters." *U.S. News & World Report,* September 27, 1993, 68-71.

Shapiro, Laura. "Why Women Are Angry." *Newsweek,* October 21, 1991, 41-44.

Sommers, Christina Hoff. *Who Stole Feminism?* New York: Simon & Schuster, 1994.

_____. "Figuring Out Feminism." *National Review,* June 27, 1994, 30-34.

Watkins, Susan Alice; Marisa Rueda; and Marta Rodriguez. *Introducing Feminism.* Cambridge, England: Icon Books Ltd., 1994.

Wolf, Naomi. *Fire With Fire: The New Female Power and How It Will Change the 21st Century.* New York: Random House, 1993.

_____. "Can You Be a Feminist and Love Men Too?" *Cosmopolitan,* May 1994, 202-204.

Wright, Lawrence. "Women & Men." *Utne Reader,* January/February 1993, 53-61.

Index

Members of the National Organization for Women paraded in Atlantic City, New Jersey, in 1974. The Miss America pageant was held in Atlantic City the same week, drawing many feminist protesters.

Acknowledgments

Photographs used with permission of © Richard B. Levine: pp. 2, 6, 10, 63; UPI / Bettmann: pp. 9, 13, 37, 95; © Shmuel Thaler: pp. 14, 43; The Bettmann Archive: pp. 19, 20, 24, 27, 30; Archive Photos / Waton: pp. 28–29; Archive Photos / Fotos International: p. 32; Reuters / Bettmann: pp. 35, 72, 73, 75; Archive Photos / SAGA / Capri: pp. 39, 76; © Frances M. Roberts: pp. 42, 47, 79; Archive Photos / Howard: p. 44; © Luca Babini: p. 54; Joyce Ravid: p. 57; Oklahoma State University: p. 58; Jerry Bauer: p. 64; Archive Photos / Consolidated News: p. 71.

Cover photograph: © Richard B. Levine

About the Author

JoAnn Bren Guernsey has published three young adult novels and coauthored a mystery series dealing with environmental issues. Her recently published nonfiction books address topics such as teen pregnancy, rape, abortion, animal rights, and capital punishment. She is an active member of the Society of Children's Book Writers and Illustrators and a contributer to Lerner's Pro/Con series.

Guernsey lives in St. Paul, Minnesota, with her two teenage daughters, who love to debate—with her and everyone else—the issues addressed in her books.

Learn more about issues in the news through Lerner's Frontline series:

AIDS: *Examining the Crisis*

Sexual Harassment: *A Question of Power*

Youth Violence: *An American Epidemic?*